Katie Woo

Daddy Can't Dance

by Fran Manushkin

illustrated by Tammie Lyon

PICTURE WINDOW BOOKS
a capstone imprint

Katie Woo is published by Picture Window Books,
A Capstone Imprint
1710 Roe Crest Drive
North Mankato, Minnesota 56003
www.capstonepub.com

Library of Congress Cataloging-in-Publication Data
Names: Manushkin, Fran, author.
Title: Daddy can't dance / by Fran Manushkin.
Other titles: Daddy cannot dance
Description: North Mankato, Minnesota: Picture Window Books/
    Capstone Press, [2018] | Series: Katie Woo | Summary: Katie and her
    father are invited to a Daddy-Daughter dance, the only problem is
    that her father is not a good dancer — he frequently steps on his
    partner's feet.
Identifiers: LCCN 2017031065 (print) | LCCN 2017031879 (ebook) |
    ISBN 9781515822707 (eBook PDF) | ISBN 9781515822721 (reflowable
    Epub) | ISBN 9781515822660 (hardcover) | ISBN 9781515822684 (pbk.)
Subjects: LCSH: Woo, Katie (Fictitious character)—Juvenile fiction. |
    Chinese Americans—Juvenile fiction. | Fathers and daughters—Juvenile
    fiction. | Dance parties—Juvenile fiction. | CYAC: Chinese Americans—
    Fiction. | Fathers and daughters—Fiction. | Dance parties—Fiction.
Classification: LCC PZ7.M3195 (ebook) | LCC PZ7.M3195 Dad 2018
    (print) | DDC 813.54 [E] — dc23
LC record available at https://lccn.loc.gov/2017031065

Graphic Designer: Ted Williams

Printed and bound in the USA.
010765S18

Table of Contents

Chapter 1

The Daddy-Daughter Dance

"Look at this letter," said

Katie's dad. "We are invited

to a dance."

"Cool!" said Katie. "Is

it a ballet? I love to watch

ballet."

"It's a daddy-daughter dance," said her father. "*We* will be dancing."

"Cool!" said Katie, twirling around. "I'm a good dancer."

"I'm a good dancer too," said Katie's dad. "I'm good at stepping on your mom's toes."

"For sure!" said Katie's mom.

"Don't worry," Katie told her dad. "We have lots of time. I can teach you."

"Great," said her dad. "I want you to be proud of me."

Chapter 2

Daddy's Dance Moves

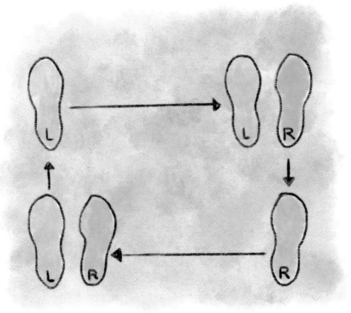

"Let's start with a slow

dance," said Katie. "See how

I am dancing in a square?"

"I see," said her dad.

Katie's dad put his arms around Katie. He smiled and said, "So far, so good."

Then they began dancing.

After two steps, Katie

yelled, "Ouch! You stepped

on my foot."

"Sorry!" said her dad.

"Let's try again," said
Katie.

Oops! She tripped over
her dad's foot.

"Your feet are big," said
Katie. "Dancing with you
is tricky."

"I can do a fast dance,"

said her father. "See? Nobody's

toes get in the way."

Katie's mom danced too.

She was awesome.

The next day, Pedro
came over. He was a terrific
dancer.

"I love to kick when I
dance," he said. "It's like
playing soccer."

"You can't kick in a slow dance," said Katie. "I will be wearing a fancy dress, and a slow dance is dreamy."

A few days later, JoJo
and Katie went shopping
for fancy dresses.

"The blue dress is pretty,"
said Katie. "But this red dress
is dreamier. I pick red."

But on the day of the
dance, Katie told her dad,
"Maybe I should have
picked the blue dress."

"No way," said her dad.
"Red is a lucky color. I even
got a tie to match it."

Chapter 3

The Big Night

At the gym, Katie and her dad said hi to Yoko and her uncle and Mattie and her grandpa.

"Cool dress," said Mattie.

Katie smiled and said, "Red is the color of luck."

The first dance was a fast one. "I can do that," said Katie's dad. He was terrific.

JoJo and her dad waved at them. The gym was rocking!

Then a slow dance started.

Katie's dad looked worried.

He said, "Let's rest now."

So they sat down and

watched the dreamy dancers.

"My new shoes feel tight,"
said Katie. She took them off
to wiggle her toes.

Katie looked at her
bare feet and her dad's big,
hard shoes. "Ha!" she said.
"I have an idea."

"This is how we can do a slow dance," said Katie. "I'll dance on your feet!"

"Wow!" He smiled. "I can *do* this."

They danced and danced.

Katie's dad felt proud.

So did Katie.

"What a cool idea," said

Katie's friends. They danced

on toes too.

When they got home,

Katie and her dad showed

her mom their dance.

"Lovely!" said Katie's

mom.

Before bedtime, Katie

hugged her dress and did

a few last spins.

She felt very lucky!

About the Author

Fran Manushkin is the author of many popular picture books, including *Happy in Our Skin*; *Baby, Come Out!*; *Latkes and Applesauce: A Hanukkah Story*; *The Tushy Book*; *Big Girl Panties*; *Big Boy Underpants*; and *Bamboo for Me, Bamboo for You*. There is a real Katie Woo — she's Fran's great-niece — but she never gets in half the trouble of the Katie Woo in the books. Fran writes on her beloved Mac computer in New York City, without the help of her two naughty cats, Chaim and Goldy..

About the Illustrator

Tammie Lyon began her love for drawing at a young age while sitting at the kitchen table with her dad. She continued her love of art and eventually attended the Columbus College of Art and Design, where she earned a bachelor's degree in fine art. After a brief career as a professional ballet dancer, she decided to devote herself full-time to illustration. Today she lives with her husband, Lee, in Cincinnati, Ohio. Her dogs, Gus and Dudley, keep her company as she works in her studio.

Glossary

awesome (AW-suhm)—causing a feeling of admiration or wonder

ballet (bal-LAY)—a performance that uses dance and music, often to tell a story

dreamy (DREE-mee)—quiet and soothing

proud (PROUD)—happy or satisfied with what you or someone else has achieved

terrific (tuh-RIF-ik)—very good or excellent

tricky (TRIK-ee)—difficult in an unexpected way

twirling (TWURL-ing)—turning or spinning around quickly

wiggle (WIG-uhl)—to make small movements from side to side

Let's Talk

1. Talk about the different ways dancing is described in the story.

2. What was Katie's dad's dancing problem? How did Katie solve it? Would her solution work with a dancer her own age? Why or why not?

3. Who do you think was the best dancer in this story? Why?

Let's Write

1. Make a poster to tell people about the daddy-daughter dance. Be sure to include when and where it is happening.

2. Write about a time you did something special with your dad, uncle, grandpa, or another special man.

3. The daddy-daughter dance was a fancy party. Draw a picture of what you would wear to a fancy party, and write a few sentences describing your outfit.

Having Fun with Katie Woo!

Sometimes men wear small flowers on their jackets for special occasions. They are called boutonnieres (pronounced boo-tuhn-EERS). You can make your own boutonniere out of tissue paper and give it to your special guy!

Fabulous Flowers

What you need:

- colorful tissue paper

- scissors

- green pipe cleaners

- marker

- small cup

What you do:

1. Layer the tissue paper until you have 8 to 12 layers together.

2. Lay the cup on the paper. Using the marker, trace the cup to make a circle.

3. Cut out the circle, cutting through all the layers of tissue paper.

4. Using the tip of the scissors make two small circles, about an inch apart, in the center of the circle.

5. Insert a pipe cleaner through one hole. Then loop it down into the second hole. Twist the pipe cleaner around itself so it is secure. This is your stem.

6. Layer by layer, scrunch the paper up, scrunching it in slightly different directions with each layer. This is your flower!

7. If needed, trim the pipe cleaner so it is about 4 inches long. You can also shape a leaf out of another piece of pipe cleaner and twist it around the stem to secure.

THE FUN DOESN'T STOP HERE!

Discover more at www.capstonekids.com

💜 Videos & Contests

✿ Games & Puzzles

💜 Friends & Favorites

✿ Authors & Illustrators

Find cool websites and more books like this one at www.facthound.com. Just type in the Book ID: **9781515822660** and you're ready to go!